Barbie through the Decades

DiscoverRoo

An Imprint of Pop!
popbooksonline.com

Barbie Today

by Elizabeth Andrews

WELCOME TO DiscoverRoo!

This book is filled with videos, puzzles, games, and more! Scan the QR codes* while you read, or visit the website below to make this book pop.

popbooksonline.com/today

abdobooks.com

Published by Pop!, a division of ABDO, PO Box 398166, Minneapolis, Minnesota 55439.

Printed in the United States of America, North Mankato, Minnesota.

052024
082024

THIS BOOK CONTAINS RECYCLED MATERIALS

Cover Photo: MATTEL/SIPA/Newscom

Interior Photos: Getty Images, Shutterstock Images, Wikimedia, Design Bay Productions, Alamy Stock Photo, Mattel/Mega/Newscom/IBLIM, Mattel/Mega/Newscom/GWGLA, Cover Images/ZUMAPRESS/Newscom, Simon Webb/ZUMAPRESS/Newscom, Mattel/MEGA/Newscom/CJMAR, Michael Bowles/ZUMAPRESS/Newscom

Editor: Grace Hansen

Series Designer: Victoria Bates

Library of Congress Control Number: 2023947582

Publisher's Cataloging-in-Publication Data

Names: Andrews, Elizabeth, author.

Title: Barbie today / by Elizabeth Andrews

Description: Minneapolis, Minnesota : Pop!, 2025 | Series: Barbie through the decades | Includes online resources and index

Identifiers: ISBN 9781098246303 (lib. bdg.) | ISBN 9781098246860 (ebook)

Subjects: LCSH: Barbie dolls--Juvenile literature. | Toys--History--Juvenile literature. | History, Modern--Juvenile literature. | Toys--Social aspects--Juvenile literature. | Popular Culture--Juvenile literature.

Classification: DDC 688.722--dc23

*Scanning QR codes requires a web-enabled smart device with a QR code reader app and a camera.

TABLE OF Contents

CHAPTER 1

Barbie's Beginnings

Humans have made dolls for thousands of years. At first, dolls were made of clay, straw, or other natural materials. As the world changed, so did dolls. The toys got more detailed and exciting. In 1959, the fashion doll, Barbie, hit store shelves. The doll game was never the same.

WATCH A VIDEO HERE!

Barbie's original striped swimsuit was inspired by fashions worn in the 1950s.

Ruth Handler was the creator of Barbie. Ruth and her husband owned the toy company Mattel Creations. Ruth noticed that children's dolls were mostly baby dolls. She believed growing girls didn't want to play with babies. They wanted dolls that encouraged them to dream of their futures.

Ruth Handler was born in Denver, Colorado, in 1916.

Mattel released the first Barbie in 1959. She wore a black-and-white swimsuit, black high heels, white sunglasses, and gold earrings. Barbie was a teenage fashion model from Willows, Wisconsin. She cost $3. Her extra outfits ranged between $1 and $5.

The Handler family

DID YOU KNOW?

Barbie's full name is Barbara Millicent Roberts. She was named after Ruth's daughter Barbara.

The first Barbie commercial played during an episode of The Mickey Mouse Club.

Barbie was a hit! In the first year, Mattel sold 350,000 dolls. Soon customers were asking for more. Mattel went on to create friends, dreamhouses, cars, and more than 250 careers for Barbie. Ruth was right. Children did like grown-up dolls. Their imaginations grew with Barbie!

The first Barbie appeared passive and gentle. She fit into the late 1950s female tradition of **homemaking** and beauty **trends**. Some of the first Barbies included Barbie Learns to Cook and Suburban Shopper Barbie. However, Ruth wouldn't keep Barbie in the home for long.

Suburban Shopper Barbie, 1959

CHAPTER 2

Living in the Real World

A new generation of women is emerging today! In the 2020s, girls and boys are often raised by mothers who feel passionate about women's rights in the workplace and society. Female role models often hold high-power positions at work. They own their own businesses and care for their families.

LEARN MORE HERE!

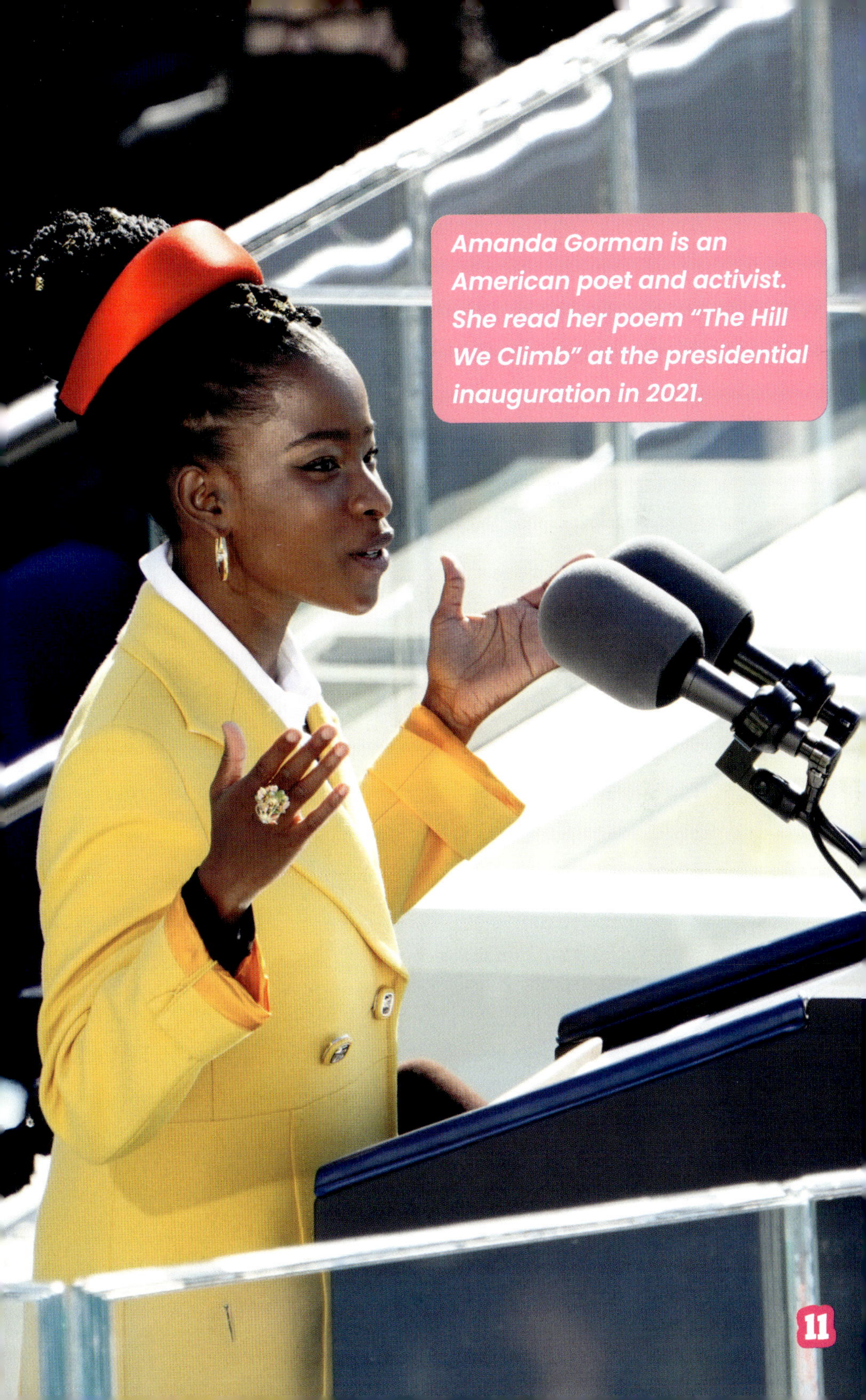

Amanda Gorman is an American poet and activist. She read her poem "The Hill We Climb" at the presidential inauguration in 2021.

In the 2010s and into the 2020s, another women's rights movement began. This time it focused on the poor treatment women faced in the workplace by their male coworkers. In 2017, the hashtag #MeToo took social media by storm. Women were sharing similar experiences. Many powerful men in Hollywood and world politics were exposed for their actions.

Many people showed support for women's rights by wearing #MeToo themed clothes.

#BlackLivesMatter protesters host marches to call for the fair treatment of Black people.

#BlackLivesMatter began in 2013 after Trayvon Martin, an unarmed, 17-year-old, was killed. Black Lives Matter is now a social movement. It gains more attention every year as injustices are revealed to the public through the news and social media. The movement exposed **racism** in society and the **criminal justice system**.

Climate activists inspire people to fight climate change.

Climate change became more noticeable in the 2010s. Today, fires, floods, heatwaves, and other natural disasters are more common. Coral reefs are dying. People around the world are asking governments and businesses to focus on caring for the environment.

DID YOU KNOW?

Scientists have created many projects to clean and heal the ocean. One project works to regrow coral reefs!

Social media is constantly evolving. Instagram, TikTok, Youtube, and X (formerly Twitter) are some of the most used sites. People of all ages share their lives and experiences online. Information is exchanged immediately. Global disasters and victories can be seen from around the world on a smart phone screen.

Young people can stay connected to friends through their phones.

CHAPTER 3

Barbie's New Look

Mattel knew the Barbie Universe (BU) needed a shake up. Its sales dropped 20 percent between 2012 and 2014. Mattel sent out a survey asking the public what changes they wanted to see. The answer was clear. People wanted Barbie to be more relatable.

EXPLORE LINKS HERE!

In 2015, Mattel released three new Barbie body types. The company added tall, petite, and curvy Barbies. Barbie also came with new hair types and skin colors. Dolls in wheelchairs, with down syndrome, and with **prosthetic** limbs also joined the BU.

Some Barbies have vitiligo. This is a condition that causes patches of skin to lose color.

DID YOU KNOW?

More than 1 billion people in the world experience a disability.

As kids were spending more time on the internet, so did Barbie. Mattel created a social media presence for Barbie on Instagram and X. Barbie's official Instagram has more than 3 million followers. Fans follow her for fashion and lifestyle advice.

Barbie has lived in many dreamhouses. In 2021, Mattel released a content-ready house. It was inspired by the homes of social media stars. This new dreamhouse had places for Barbie to record videos and take pictures. It also had an elevator, so all of Barbie's friends could take part in the fun.

Barbie got her first dreamhouse in 1962! It was much smaller and simpler than the 2021 version.

Barbie the movie, directed by Greta Gerwig, was released in 2023. Margot Robbie, Ryan Gosling, America Ferrera, and more superstars brought the classic dolls, such as Barbie and Ken, to life. The movie covers important topics such as girlhood and the importance of equality for men and women. It was a hit and inspired new and old Barbie fans alike.

Mattel released dolls inspired by the movie!

Barbie The Movie

The Barbie movie was released July 21, 2023. It made $1.4 billion. Barbie was the highest-earning movie in 2023.

The Barbie movie had many important lessons. One lesson it taught was that even though life can be hard, girls can do anything! When life got hard in Barbieland, the Barbies worked together to make it better. Friendship and acceptance helped the heroes of the movie solve the problems in Barbieland.

CHAPTER 4

Barbie Forever

Today, Barbie wants to shine a light on important, real-life female role models. Professional skateboarder Sky Brown was made into a Barbie when she was 12 years old. Ibtihaj Muhammad was the first American to compete in the Olympics wearing a **hijab**. Mattel created a Barbie in her likeness in 2018 as part of the Shero collection.

COMPLETE AN ACTIVITY HERE!

Muslim girls who wear headscarves could see themselves in the Ibtihaj Muhammad Barbie doll.

Healthcare workers were on the front lines of the fight against COVID-19.

Mattel has always tried to inspire girls to take on careers that were more often held by men. Barbie has had many jobs in **STEM** including an astronaut and a surgeon. **Conservationist** Jane Goodall and space scientist Dr. Maggie Aderin-Pocock are Barbie dolls. Nurses and doctors who helped fight COVID-19 became dolls too.

Mattel introduced the Barbie Loves the Ocean collection in 2021. These dolls were made from recycled ocean-bound plastic. Mattel is working hard to make their toys safe for the environment to help fight **climate change**. The collection included three dolls and a beach shack play set.

Ocean-bound plastic is plastic waste at risk of ending up in the ocean.

On Barbie's YouTube channel, she shares her daily life and adventures. The channel has nearly 12 million followers. One of Barbie's most important videos discusses **racism**. In 2015, Barbie talked with her friend Nikki who is a person of color. Together they inspired their followers to listen and take a stand against racism.

Campaign Manager, Presidential Candidate, Fundraiser, and Voter Barbie (left to right), *2020*

Barbie "Brooklyn" Stylist works in wardrobe and costume design at a fashion shoot!

Barbie in Brooklyn

In 2021, Barbie "Brooklyn" Roberts was introduced in a YouTube video. Mattel wanted to make sure Black girls could see themselves as lead characters. Barbie "Brooklyn" lives in New York City. She likes to cook with her dad and learn about her family history. Now, both Barbies share the YouTube channel.

Mattel released a Barbie wearing a hearing aid (left) in 2022!

Mattel always wanted Barbie to serve as a role model for children. After learning that kids couldn't see themselves in Barbie anymore, Mattel made important changes. Barbie is a symbol of fashion, hard work, and strength. She will help build dreams forever!

Space scientist Dr. Maggie Aderin-Pocock, 2023

Making Connections

TEXT-TO-SELF

Have you ever played with Barbie or her friends? If so, what kind of life did you imagine for them? If not, what kind of life would you imagine?

TEXT-TO-TEXT

Have you read any books about other toys? What did those toys have in common with Barbie? How were they different?

TEXT-TO-WORLD

Mattel made many important changes to the Barbie Universe between 2010 and today. The changes were made to better reflect the real world. What are some other changes Barbie could make to help every person feel included?

Glossary

climate change — a long-term change in Earth's climate. It includes changing temperatures, weather patterns, and more.

conservationist — a person who takes action to care for and protect nature.

criminal justice system — the systems within the government that are responsible for stopping or discouraging crime.

hijab — a covering for the hair and neck that is worn by some Muslim women.

homemaking — caring for a household by cooking, cleaning, and raising children.

prosthetic — an artificial device to replace a missing or impaired part of the body

racism — the belief that one race is better than another.

STEM — science, technology, engineering, and mathematics.

trend — a current style or preference especially concerning clothing.

Index